Dear Parents and Educators,

Welcome to Penguin Young Readers! As parents and educators, you know that each child develops at their own pace—in terms of speech, critical thinking, and, of course, reading. Penguin Young Readers recognizes this fact. As a result, each Penguin Young Readers book is assigned a traditional easy-to-read level (1–4) as well as an F&P Text Level (A–P). Both of these systems will help you choose the right book for your child. Please refer to the back of each book for specific leveling information. Penguin Young Readers features esteemed authors and illustrators, stories about favorite characters, fascinating nonfiction, and more!

Dirt and Bugsy: Beetle Mania

LEVEL **2**

F&P TEXT LEVEL **I**

This book is perfect for a **Progressing Reader** who:
- can figure out unknown words by using picture and context clues;
- can recognize beginning, middle, and ending sounds;
- can make and confirm predictions about what will happen in the text; and
- can distinguish between fiction and nonfiction.

Here are some **activities** you can do during and after reading this book:
- Picture Clues: Use the pictures to tell the story. Try going through the story again from beginning to end, using the pictures to retell the story in your own words.
- Make Predictions: Dirt and Bugsy love to collect and sort beetles. What other bugs could they collect and how should they sort them?

Remember, sharing the love of reading with a child is the best gift you can give!

*This book has been officially leveled by using the F&P Text Level Gradient™ leveling system.

For Wake and Brendan, who catch
all kinds of cool bugs—ML

To Mom, Dad, and Shay: thank you for your
constant and unending support and love.
P.S. Thanks for not yelling at me when
I drew on the wall, Momma—SLP

PENGUIN YOUNG READERS
An imprint of Penguin Random House LLC, New York

First published in the United States of America by Penguin Young Readers,
an imprint of Penguin Random House LLC, New York, 2023

Text copyright © 2023 by Megan Litwin
Illustrations copyright © 2023 by Penguin Random House LLC

Visit us online at penguinrandomhouse.com.

Library of Congress Cataloging-in-Publication Data is available.

Manufactured in China

ISBN 9780593519943 (pbk)   10 9 8 7 6 5 4 3 2 1 WKT
ISBN 9780593519950 (hc)   10 9 8 7 6 5 4 3 2 1 WKT

PENGUIN YOUNG READERS

LEVEL

PROGRESSING
READER

2

Dirt and Bugsy
Beetle Mania

by Megan Litwin

illustrated by Shauna Lynn Panczyszyn

Dirt and Bugsy are

bug catchers.

They catch all kinds of bugs.

Bugs that crawl.

Bugs that fly.

Bugs that slide.

Bugs that hide.

Today they are looking for beetles.

It is not very hard.

Beetles are everywhere.

On the ground

and in the air.

Their jars are soon crawling
with beetles.
All kinds of beetles.

Black beetles.

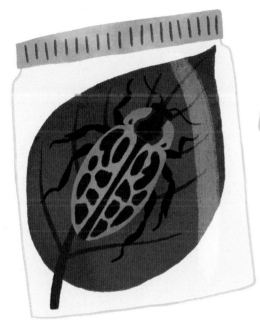

Spotted beetles.

Tiny beetles.

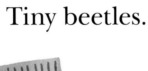

Shiny beetles.

But what to do with all the beetles?

The bug boys think.

Their brains buzz.

They come up
with a plan.

They will sort
the beetles.
Sorting is fun.

11

Bugsy runs to find some hoops.

Dirt goes to get
some chalk.

And then they begin.

Bugsy wants to sort by color.

Red, black, blue, green.

Dirt wants to sort by size.

Big, small, in-between.

The boys cannot agree.

Which way is best?

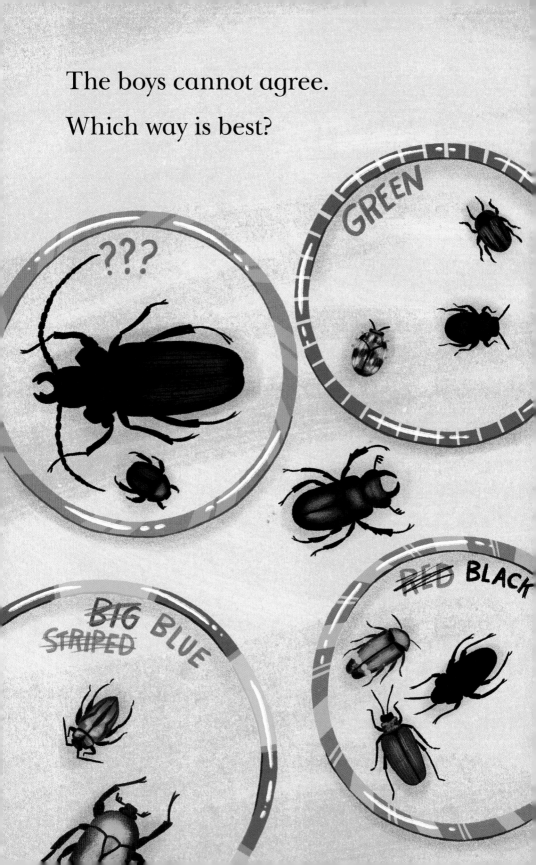

They each try their own way.

But soon the bugs are all mixed-up.

17

Some beetles
have stripes.

And some
have spots.

Some seem small.

But they are not!

Dirt and Bugsy are going buggy.

Sorting is harder than catching.

BUZZ, go the beetles.
BUZZ, go their brains.

Until they get a new idea.

This time, the bug boys agree.

There is so much to love
about beetles!

The sorting is done.

Now for more fun.

And when the day is done,
the bugs go home.

Colors flash.

Wings flap.

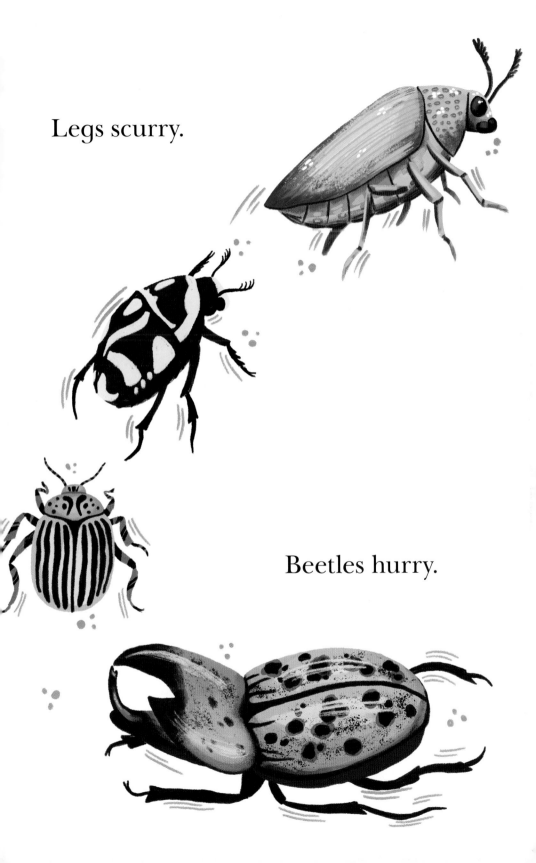

Legs scurry.

Beetles hurry.

Beetles, beetles everywhere.

On the ground and in the air.

"Goodbye, goodbye!" Bugsy calls after them.

"Catch you later," says Dirt.

And they will.

Dirt and Bugsy are good
bug catchers.
They catch all kinds of bugs.

Again, and again, and again . . .

Beautiful Beetles

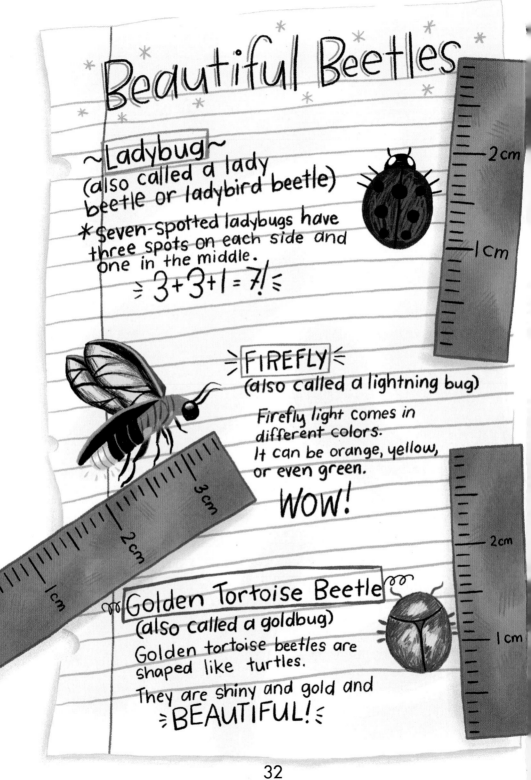

~Ladybug~
(also called a lady beetle or ladybird beetle)

*Seven-spotted ladybugs have three spots on each side and one in the middle.

$$3 + 3 + 1 = 7!$$

FIREFLY
(also called a lightning bug)

Firefly light comes in different colors.
It can be orange, yellow, or even green.

WOW!

Golden Tortoise Beetle
(also called a goldbug)

Golden tortoise beetles are shaped like turtles.

They are shiny and gold and
BEAUTIFUL!